FIND THE ANIMAL

GOD MADE SOMETHING BEAUTIFUL

This squirrel knows what animal we are looking for. Can you find this squirrel in the book?

PENNY REEVE
ILLUSTRATED BY ROGER DE KLERK

C F 4 • K

Let's go on an adventure. What will we find? It's something God has made. It's something beautiful!

Can you find the rabbits?

This is what I seek, to gaze upon the beauty of the Lord. Psalm 27:4

Where is the red toadstool?

What could this be? It's an eye. How many eyes can you see? God made these eyes very beautiful.

Can you find the tiny, little bird?

God has made everything beautiful.
Ecclesiastes 3:11

Is the boy's T-shirt blue or red?

What is this? It's a wing. How many wings can you see? This animal does not always fly, but God gave it beautiful wings.

Can you find the blue butterfly?

God saw all that he had made and it was very good. Genesis 1:31

Is the girl's dress yellow or orange?

What about this? It is a feather. How many feathers can you see? God made these feathers lovely and soft.

Can you find the little snail?

God's work is perfect.
Deuteronomy 32:4

Is the girl's hairband blue or is it red?

And what is this? It's a tail. How many colours are on the tail? This tail is like a big and beautiful fan. God made this tail to be looked at.

Can you find the camera?

Great is the Lord, and most worthy of praise.
Psalm 48:1

Where is the brown deer?

Which animal have we found? It is something beautiful. It is a peacock. Who made it? Our great God!

Can you find the blue bird?

The law of the Lord is perfect. Psalm 19:7

Who has a purple pencil?

A peacock is beautiful. Our God is beautiful. We cannot see him but he is still beautiful because he is loving, and faithful and perfect!

Can you find the pink flower?

Every good and perfect gift is from God. James 1:17

Where is the red squirrel?

Thank you God, for being so beautiful. You loved me so
much you sent your Son to die for me.
Thank you Jesus for doing this. Help me to love you more.

Jesus said, 'Your Heavenly Father is perfect.'
Matthew 5:48.